The Berenstain Bears®

ALL YEAR 'ROUND

Stan & Jan Berenstain

A GOLDEN BOOK • NEW YORK

Western Publishing Company, Inc., Racine, Wisconsin 53404

In winter
we are always told
to put on hats
or we'll get cold.

When we go out,
we see our breath.
We see our friends
Fred and Beth.

The snow and ice
are really great!
We can sled!
We can skate!

5

Mama can do
a figure eight.
Hooray for Mama!
Isn't she great?

Papa, stop!

That ice is thin.

Don't skate there.

You may fall in!

Soon signs of spring
begin to show.
Bits of green
grow through the snow.

Crocuses
begin to peep,
waking from
their winter sleep.

We see one with
a yellow face.
We see robins find
a nesting place.

They build a nest
of grass and twigs.

Then Daddy Robin
digs and digs.

He digs for worms
in our yard.
The ground is still
cold and hard.

He finds a worm!
He gets lucky!

You may think that
worms are yucky.

But to robins
they are yummy!
Just right for
a robin's tummy!

The sun climbs higher
in the sky.
Mom says spring's
the reason why.

We get out bikes.

We put back sleds.

Mama weeds
the flower beds.

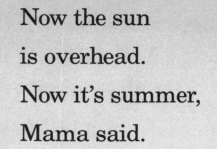

Now the sun
is overhead.
Now it's summer,
Mama said.

Flowers!
How their colors glow!

You can almost
see them grow!

Minute by minute!
Hour by hour!
Summer's the season
of FLOWER POWER!

Mama makes some
lemonade.

We will drink it
in the shade.

Here's the lake
where we all swim.
Brother's slow.
I yell at him.

Come on, Brother!
Shake a leg!
Last one in
is a rotten egg!

We swim.

We float.

We wave to someone
in a boat.

We see a fish.

We see a frog.

Look! Is that an alligator?

No. It's just a floating log!

Come out, says Mama.
You've had enough!

The clouds float by,
puff by puff.

We feel the sun
on our backs.
We eat wild berries
for our snacks.

We feel a breeze.
It's getting cool.
We'll soon be going
back to school.

Summertime
is almost gone.
The seasons just keep
moving on.

The color of leaves
turns bright and bold.

Yellow!   Red!

Orange!

Gold!

Fall is here!
It's all around!
Leaves are falling
to the ground!

28

Most flowers are gone.

But we still have some.

This one's called

chry-san-the-mum.

Winter's coming.
And we all know
what trees stay green
in the snow!

Christmas trees
remind us, friends,
that very soon
the whole year ends.

But you and we
will still be here,
all set to start
a brand-new year!